®
From the Land of Serendipity™...
your own keepsake bookmark.
PRICE STERN SLOAN
Los Angeles

NAPOLEON'S RAINBOW

Written and illustrated
by Robin James

A Serendipity™ Book

PRICE STERN SLOAN
Los Angeles

The Serendipity™ series was created by
Stephen Cosgrove and Robin James.

Published by Price Stern Sloan, Inc.
A member of The Putnam & Grosset Group

ISBN: 0-8431-3610-3

Library of Congress Catalog Card Number: 93-86094

10 9 8 7 6 5 4 3 2 1

Dedicated to Jessica Irene James, who loves purple even more than I do.

—Auntie Robin

On the Island of Serendipity, at the edge of a tiny forest is a place called Rainbow Glen. Many different kinds of creatures live and play there. And every day when the sun shines bright, its rays filter through the mist of waterfalls, turning everything in Rainbow Glen every glorious color of the rainbow.

Everyone who lived in this beautiful place loved colors. And each family seemed to have their own special favorite. The Lemoninskys had a darling saffron house with bright yellow shutters on the windows and a canary-colored mailbox. Their front porch railing was made of golden oak and the flower beds were full of daffodils and buttercups.

Farther down the lane, in a cute little green house, lived the MacEmeralds. Their house had lime green trim and chartreuse shingles on the roof. All around their yard was a fence made of olive leaves, and of course their grass was the greenest in the neighborhood.

The Bluebinkles' house was next down the lane. It was quite a sight. The entry was paved with royal blue slate, forget-me-nots lined the walkway, and a wreath made of blueberries hung from the powder-blue front door.

From the O'Crimsons to the Orangebies, the Pinkmans to the McMauves, everyone in the neighborhood took great pride in their homes. It really didn't matter what color a family liked, as long as everything in each home matched.

All the neighbors were close friends. They often went to each others' houses but only for short visits. If they stayed too long, their colors might clash.

Rainbow Glen was a harmonious community, except for one problem. This problem was Napoleon Pavonine.

Napoleon lived all alone at the very end of Crayon Lane, in a small dark house with absolutely no sense of color. But Napoleon, himself, was every color of the rainbow. Even worse, he didn't seem to match anything. Napoleon was so different that none of the neighbors had the nerve to go near him.

One day when Mr. Lemoninsky was out in his yard proudly pruning his buttercups, Mr. MacEmerald walked over to chat. He had a concern about the newcomers who had just moved in.

"What are we going to do about that awful Mr. Pavonine?" he asked. "You know the new neighbors have a little one. If she wanders from home and gets too close to Napoleon's house… I would hate to think what might happen. Do you think we should warn them?"

"Yes, we'd better," said Mr. Lemoninsky. And they headed across the street.

The newest neighbors were the Purps. They had just moved into a lovely lavender home with plum curtains. Violets bloomed in neat little rows on either side of their lilac front door. Mrs. Purp was busy baking a nice plum pudding when she heard the doorbell ring.

"We just wanted to warn you about Napoleon Pavonine who lives down the lane near the woods," said Mr. Lemoninsky.

"Yes," said Mr. MacEmerald, "He is very strange. He mixes all his colors together and doesn't even HAVE a favorite color! If I were you, I'd stay as far away from him as possible."

"Thank you for telling me," said Mrs. Purp. "We will certainly take your advice."

The next morning, little Phoebe Purp put on the perfectly matched outfit her mother had laid out for her. It was Phoebe's favorite, a pretty mulberry dress with a sparkling amethyst clip for her hair.

Phoebe never picked out her own clothes because she saw colors differently than anyone else. To her, green was red and blue was yellow. If her outfits were left to her, she'd dress in every color of the rainbow.

Phoebe took one last twirl before the mirror and headed downstairs. After breakfast, her parents told her all about strange old Mr. Pavonine who lived down the lane.

"But why is he so awful?" asked Phoebe.

Mr. and Mrs. Purp looked at each other and said, "Because everyone says so." They left it at that and warned her not to go near his house. Phoebe listened carefully and went out the door.

Heeding her parents' warning, Phoebe took a different route to school, through the woods. The only problem was that she wasn't quite used to it. And that afternoon, on the way back home, Phoebe got very lost.

She climbed over logs and pushed her way through the bushes. Brambles grabbed at her feet and tore at her hair. It was starting to get dark and Phoebe was frightened. Try as she might, she couldn't find her way out of the woods.

In a panic, she started to run. Something caught her foot and the next thing Phoebe knew, she was flat on the ground. When she tried to get up, pain shot through her foot and she fell back down. She couldn't walk and it was getting cold—all she wanted was to get home. Phoebe began to cry.

Back in the neighborhood, Napoleon Pavonine was straightening up his little house. He wasn't color-coordinated, but he was certainly very tidy.

As he was dusting under his favorite pink lamp by the window, Napoleon heard the commotion outside. He pulled back the orange curtains to see what it was.

Everyone in Rainbow Glen was out, desperately searching under bushes, scrambling around trees, and calling, "Phoebe! Phoebe!"

Napoleon noticed Mr. and Mrs. Purp holding each other tightly and looking very frightened. Suddenly he knew what had happened.

Napoleon grabbed a quilt off his polka-dot couch and slipped quietly out the back door to look for Phoebe. He had a pretty good idea where she might be.

Napoleon didn't have to look very long before he heard faint sounds of crying. There was Phoebe crumpled among the ferns.

"You must be Phoebe Purp," said Napoleon.

"How did you know my name?" said Phoebe.

"Everyone in Rainbow Glen is calling it," he said. "They're all out looking for you."

"Really?" asked Phoebe.

Napoleon nodded. "Looks like you could use a little help getting home."

Phoebe looked up between tearful sobs. "Oh yes! Thank you! I'm lost," she said. "I was so scared. My parents told me to stay far away from Mr. Pavonine's house and before you came, I was afraid he would find me!"

Napoleon just smiled and picked Phoebe up in the blanket. She snuggled deep into the colorful folds.

"This is the most beautiful blanket I've ever seen!" she said. "It's just the way I see colors. All of them mixed up together!"

"Me too!" Napoleon laughed. "Just like a rainbow."

As Napoleon carried Phoebe home, he told her wonderful stories to keep her mind off her hurt foot. He was very nice and very funny.

The neighborhood was deserted when they arrived at Phoebe's house, but Napoleon knew the others would be back soon. He sat her gently down on the front step of her house.

"Now you just sit tight and wait here," said Napoleon.

"Thank you for bringing me home," she said reaching up to give him a sweet little kiss on the cheek. "Mr. uh, Mr.... what's your name?"

He smiled and said, "Napoleon. And you are very welcome. Good-bye now."

Phoebe watched wide-eyed as he walked away.

A few minutes later the Purps came around the corner and saw their little Phoebe sitting on the front step. They were overjoyed. They scooped her up in their arms and smothered her with hugs and kisses. Soon the whole neighborhood was huddled around the happily reunited family.

"Phoebe, where did you get this lovely blanket?" asked her mother.

"From the nice neighbor who found me in the woods," Phoebe said. "He carried me all the way home. His name is Napoleon."

"NAPOLEON!" everyone gasped.

"Could she mean Mr. Pavonine?" said Cindy O'Crimson.

"Well ... there's only one way to find out," said Mr. Purp. He picked Phoebe up in the colorful quilt and led the way to Napoleon's house.

They knocked on the door and when Napoleon opened it, Phoebe handed him the multi-colored quilt.

"Thank you for bringing our little one home safely," said Mr. Purp. "It seems we have all been very wrong about you, Napoleon. I, for one, am very sorry and would like to invite you over for some homemade grape jelly and sugar-plum scones."

"I'll bring warm buttercakes and eggnog," said Mr. Lemoninsky.

"Do you like red cherry pie?" asked Cindy O'Crimson.

"I like everything, no matter what color," said Napoleon.

So everyone gathered at the Purps. And the more stories Napoleon told, the longer everyone stayed. They had such a good time, that no one cared if their colors clashed.

From that day forward the neighborhood began to change. The Purps traded their plum curtains for the Lemoninskys' yellow ones. The Bluebinkles gave everyone forget-me-nots for their yards and the MacEmeralds passed out their prized green lawn seed. Cindy O'Crimson loved the bright purple napkins she got from the Purps and she in turn gave them her favorite scarlet teapot. From furniture to flowers, soon the entire neighborhood was a dazzling rainbow of color. It had never been so beautiful!

Thanks to Napoleon Pavonine and little Phoebe Purp, Rainbow Glen became a real rainbow.

WHEN YOU'RE USED TO SEEING THINGS
THE SAME FOR QUITE A WHILE,
TRY A CHANGE . . . YOU NEVER KNOW,
IT JUST MIGHT MAKE YOU SMILE!